THE PUPS SAVE FRIENDSHIP DAY!

Based on the teleplay written by Michael Stokes

Illustrated by MJ Illustrations

A GOLDEN BOOK • NEW YORK

randomhousekids.com

ISBN 978-1-5247-1388-1

Printed in the United States of America

10 9 8 7 6 5 4 3 2 1

It was Friendship Day in Adventure Bay, and the PAW Patrol pups were excited! On this day, everyone got to tell their friends how much they liked them.

While Marshall painted friendship cards for everyone in town, Ryder, Rocky, and Skye busily decorated the Lookout.

"I love Friendship Day," Skye said as she hung a festive banner. "It's just so . . . friendly!"

When the friendship cards were finished, Marshall loaded them onto Rubble's Digger. On their way to find Mr. Postman, they passed a spooky old house.

Rubble whispered, "A friend of a friend of a friend told me a creepy critter lives there."

Something scratched at the rickety fence, and the pups sped away.

The pups found Mr. Postman in town talking to Mayor Goodway. They gave him the cards to take to their friends.

"It would be my *dee*-light to *dee*-liver them!" Mr. Postman exclaimed.

"These cards prove that Adventure Bay is the friendliest town around!" said Mayor Goodway.

Just then, Mayor Humdinger of Foggy Bottom walked up with a kitten from the Kit-tastrophe Crew.

"We have some friendship cards that need delivering, too," he said.

The kitten launched a flurry of hat-shaped cards at Mr. Postman, and he fell down.

"My ankle!" he exclaimed. "How will I *dee*-liver all these cards to those *dee*-serving folks?"

"I guess Adventure Bay isn't the friendliest town anymore," Mayor Humdinger said.

"Adventure Bay is best-friends-forever-plus-a-hundred-years friendly!" Mayor Goodway protested.

Mayor Humdinger challenged Adventure Bay to a contest. "Whichever town comes up with the ultimate Friendship Day gift wins the title of friendliest town!" he said.

Mayor Goodway accepted the challenge.

Mayor Goodway knew she'd need Ryder and the PAW Patrol to help deliver the cards and make a great gift.

The pups went to work. Skye carried some cards to the mountains. Zuma took some out to sea. Marshall handled the rest.

Marshall's first stop was Hootie the owl's tree—
which was next to the spooky old house he'd
passed earlier!

Carrying a bag of cards, he nervously climbed his
ladder to Hootie's hole. He slipped, and the cards fell
into the yard! He was afraid to get them because he
could hear the creepy critter behind the fence.

While his friends delivered cards, Chase was given an extra-special delivery to make. Mayor Goodway had collected every cake in Mr. Porter's shop.

"I smooshed them together to make the ultimate Friendship Day gift cake," she said. "It has to get to Foggy Bottom, pronto!"

Chase was on the cake case!

Meanwhile, in Foggy Bottom, the Kit-tastrophe Crew was putting candy shaped like cabbage heads and carrots into baskets tied to helium balloons.

"What could be friendlier than sending a balloon basket of teeth-tingling candies to every person in Adventure Bay?" Mayor Humdinger said. "Especially when Foggy Bottom has all the dentists!"

But when Mayor Humdinger heard about Adventure Bay's giant gift cake, he knew he had to stop it from being delivered. He and a kitten left quickly. Bunnies came out of the bushes to eat the mayor's vegetable-shaped candies! Then they crawled into the baskets, undid the tethers, and floated away.

Mayor Humdinger and his shifty kitty put tacks
on the road to Foggy Bottom. When Chase raced
over them, he got four flat tires—and the cake
tipped over.

"This is a *cake*-tastrophe!" Chase exclaimed.
He called for help on his PupPad. Ryder and
Rocky rushed to the rescue.

Rocky quickly replaced the tires, but fixing the cake would be harder. He called for the spatula on his PupPack. "I knew this would come in handy one day," he said.

Rocky went to work reshaping the cake.

Meanwhile, bunnies in baskets filled the sky over Adventure Bay. Skye used her helicopter to gently blow them toward Chase. He launched tennis balls that carefully popped the balloons one by one. The bunnies glided to the ground and landed in Chase's net.

When Ryder saw a hat-shaped card in one basket, he had a pretty good idea where the bunnies had come from. . . .

Ryder, Chase, Rocky, and Mayor Goodway raced to Foggy Bottom.

"Perhaps you'd like to explain what you've been doing to all those bunnies," Mayor Goodway said to Mayor Humdinger.

"B-b-b-bunnies? I don't see any b-bunnies," he stammered. "I was just making you the world's biggest balloon bouquet. It's my ultimate Friendship Day gift to you and Adventure Bay. And I see you don't have a gift in return. That means I win the contest!"

Just then, Chase and Rocky rolled up with Adventure's Bay gift. Rocky had shaped the giant cake to look like Mayor Humdinger!

"That is the most beautiful thing I've ever seen," Mayor Humdinger said with a tear in his eye. "But I don't care how devastatingly handsome your cake is!" He still wanted to win the competition.

He added more balloons to his bouquet . . . and started to float away! Mayor Goodway grabbed his leg to hold him down, but she went up, too!

As they soared into the air, Mayor Humdinger said to Mayor Goodway, "You tried to save me. That's the nicest thing you or *anyone* has ever done for me."

"That's what friends do for each other," she replied.

Mayor Humdinger was amazed. "You mean you and I are . . . friends?"

"Of course," Mayor Goodway said. "But if you were a bit nicer, nice things might happen to you more often."

Mayor Humdinger said he would give it a try.

Down on the ground, Chase got his tennis-ball launcher ready to help the mayors land.

Back in Adventure Bay, Marshall and Rubble nervously walked up to the spooky house and rang the bell. The door creaked open and . . . a friendly old woman greeted them. She said her name was Miss Marjorie.

The pups sighed with relief. Miss Marjorie wasn't scary after all, and the creepy critter was actually a rambunctious raccoon named Maynard.

When Ryder met up with the pups, Marshall said, "Wouldn't making a new friend be the best way to celebrate Friendship Day?"

Rubble and Ryder agreed, so Ryder invited Miss Marjorie to help him deliver the last of the cards.

Then they all drove to the big party at the Adventure Bay town hall. Friends new and old were there—the pups, Mayor Goodway and Mayor Humdinger, Miss Marjorie, and Mr. Postman, too. Everyone agreed it was the most *paw*-some Friendship Day Adventure Bay had ever seen.